Bernard On His Own

Written and illustrated by

Syd Hoff

CLARION BOOKS
NEW YORK

For a baby bear in the old Bronx Zoo
who might now be a great-grandpa, too.

Clarion Books
a Houghton Mifflin Company imprint
215 Park Avenue South, New York, NY 10003
Text and illustrations copyright © 1993 by Syd Hoff

For information about this and other Houghton Mifflin trade and
reference books and multimedia products, visit The Bookstore
at Houghton Mifflin on the World Wide Web
at (http://www.hmco.com/trade/).

Printed in the U.S.A.

Library of Congress Cataloging-in-Publication Data

Hoff, Syd, 1912–
Bernard on his own / written and illustrated by Syd Hoff.
p.   cm.
Summary: After Bernard the bear cub tries unsuccessfully
to catch a fish, explore a cave, and play with the ducks and deer,
he receives reassurance from his father.
ISBN 0-395-65226-X   PA ISBN 0-395-79727-6
[1. Bears—Fiction.   2. Growth—Fiction.
3. Animals—Fiction.]   I. Title.
PZ7.H672Be   1993
[E]—dc20   92-21770
CIP
AC
WOZ 10 9 8 7 6 5 4 3 2

Bernard's father was busy talking with friends
about bear traps and how to stay out of them.

Bernard's mother was having a little rest
from taking care of the family.
"Maybe I can have some fun by myself,"
thought Bernard,

and he climbed up a tree—
all the way to the top.

His father had to climb up after him
and show him how to climb down.

Bernard found some honey in a beehive
and took a taste.

His mother had to save him from the bees.

"You can't go off on your own
until you can stand up
on your two hind legs,"
said Bernard's father.

"You can't go off on your own
until you can growl loud enough
for everyone in the forest to hear you,"
said his mother.

Bernard tried to stand up
on his two hind legs,
but his knees shook.

He growled as loud as he could,
but he didn't even scare a butterfly.

Bernard saw a cave between rocks.
"Bears don't stand up on their hind legs
when they sleep inside a cave,"
thought Bernard,
and he ran inside.

But the cave was so cold and dark
Bernard came running out in a hurry!

"Bears don't growl when they fish,"
thought Bernard.
"Maybe I can catch a fish for supper."

Bernard caught a fish,
but it was so slippery
he couldn't hold on to it.
"I guess I'll never be on my own,"
said Bernard sadly.

"Why don't you join us?" asked a duck.

But before he could thank her,
the ducks flew up into the air
and Bernard was left alone in the pond.

"Why don't you join us?" asked a deer.

But before Bernard could join them,

the deer went leaping through the forest
while Bernard was still on the ground.

"Who cares!" thought Bernard.

"I'm not a duck or a deer.

I'm a bear, and bears aren't afraid of anything."

And he went into the deepest part of the forest.

So many trees, and branches, and bushes!
Bernard stood up on his hind legs to look,
but he could hardly see a thing.

"Help! Help! I'm lost!" growled Bernard.

"Please, somebody, save me!"

His mother and father

came running.

"Where have you been?
We were worried about you,"
said Bernard's mother.

"Tomorrow," said Bernard's father,
"we'll show everyone how you can growl
and stand up on your hind legs."

"But right now, let's go home,"
said Bernard's mother.

"There's a nice meal of fresh berries
and honey waiting for you."

Bernard thought those were
the sweetest words he had ever heard.